Fair and Square

By Nan Holcomb

Illustrated by Dot Yoder

JASON & NORDIC PUBLISHERS
Hollidaysburg, Pennsylvania

Other Turtle Books

Buddy's Shadow

Andy Opens Wide

Sarah's Surprise

Library of Congress Cataloging-in-Publication Data

```
Holcomb, Nan, date-
  Fair and square / by Nan Holcomb: illustrated by Dot Yoder.
      p.     cm.
Summary:  Tired of others letting him win at games, Kevin, a
physically handicapped boy, learns how to win fair and square
when he competes against a computer.
  ISBN 0-944727-10-7 (hardcover).ISBN 0-944727-09-3 (paper)
[1. Physically handicapped--Fiction. 2. Winning and losing--
Fiction.  3.  computers--Fiction.]  I.Yoder. Dot. date- ill.
II. Title.
PZ7.H6972Fa 1992
[E]--dc20                                      92-7030 CIP
```

ISBN 0-944727-09-3
Printed in the U.S.A.

For Gillian

For Russell, Eddie and Ernie

For Elizabeth who helps so many learn
to play fair and square

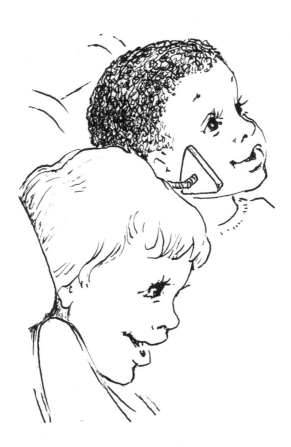

On a Friday Kevin watched Grandpa and Grandma play a game.

"Nine and nine make eighteen and two more are twenty! I won fair and square!" Grandpa said.

Grandma turned the black and white dominos over and moved them around.

"I want to play, too," Kevin said.

"I don't think you can play this game, but we'll help you play something after I beat your Grandpa," Grandma said.

"Not tonight," Mom said. "It's time for bed!"

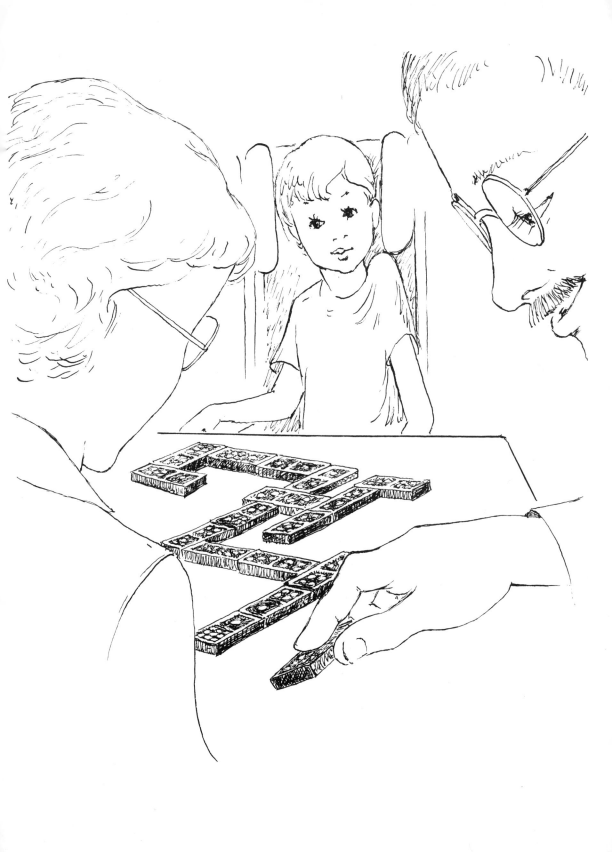

On a Saturday Kevin's brother and sister took him for a walk. They watched some boys play with radio controlled cars at the school parking lot.

The boys let Don and Jill try them.
"I want to play with the cars," Kevin said.
"No way," the kids answered. "You can't. You need to move the stick very fast."

On a Sunday Kevin watched Don and Jill play Crazy Money. "That does it!" Don said. "I beat — fair and square!"

"I want to play Crazy Money," Kevin said.

"It's too hard. You have to keep your cards secret. You can't hold them," Jill said. "We'll play Rainbow Rocket with you tomorrow."

On Monday Kevin could hardly wait until Don and Jill got home from school.

He knew he could win the game fair and square.

Jill set up the board. Don pushed Kevin to the table.

"Which piece do you want?" Jill asked.

Kevin took the blue one.

"I'll get the card for you," Jill said.

"And I'll move your blue rocket," Don said.

"But I want to play," Kevin scowled.

"You are playing. See?" Jill read the card. Don counted out the move.

Then Don and Jill took their turns. When it was Kevin's turn again, Don moved the blue piece four spaces too far.

Soon the game was over. Kevin's blue rocket was home first. Kevin howled.

"What is going on?" Mom called from the kitchen. "Did he lose?"

"No, he won!" Don and Jill answered. Kevin howled even louder.

"Then why is he crying?" Mom sat down and wiped Kevin's nose. "Why are you crying?"

"I didn't win. They cheated. I want to beat — fair and square," Kevin tried very hard to tell them.

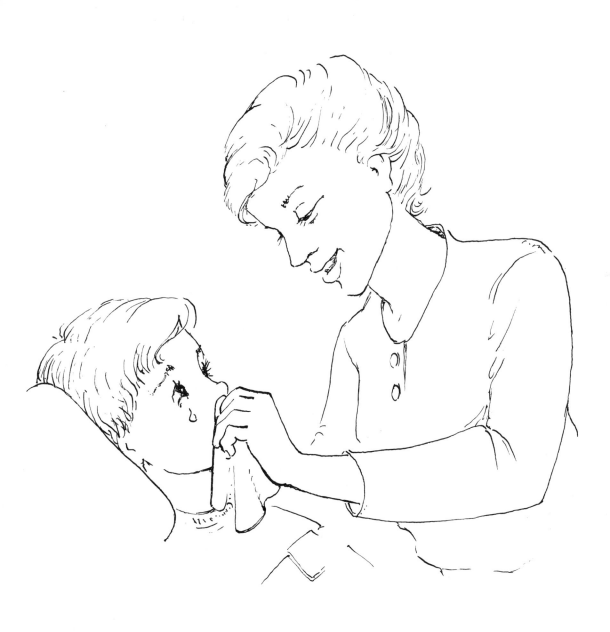

On a Tuesday Kevin went to therapy.

"Look what I have for you," Miss Wells said and put a small metal thing in front of Kevin. It had a cord that was plugged into the computer.

Miss Wells put Kevin's hand on it. "This is called a switch. Push your finger down."

Kevin pushed. A little man ran down the computer screen.

"Lift your finger up and he'll stop running," Miss Wells said. "Let's play the game together and see how you do!"

Kevin and Miss Wells played the game. Kevin lost.

In a few minutes Kevin's friend Brian came in. Brian pushed his switch with his head. They played a different game.

The rocket went very fast.

They played again.

This time Kevin won.

"Hey, I won! I really won — fair and square!"

Brian laughed and made the rocket go crazy.

On a Wednesday Miss Wells put a radio controlled car right in the middle of a small empty swimming pool. She put Kevin's hand on the switch. The car moved. It stopped. It went backward and forward. It bumped into the edges.

Miss Wells put a toy bridge and a toy tree into the pool. Kevin tried and tried. At last the car went under the bridge. Then it went around the tree.

On a Thursday the school had a play day. The boys and girls worked very hard getting ready. Kevin and Brian held the decorations until Sarah hung them up. Soon it was three o'clock.

Don, Jill, Mom, Dad, Grandpa and Grandma all came.

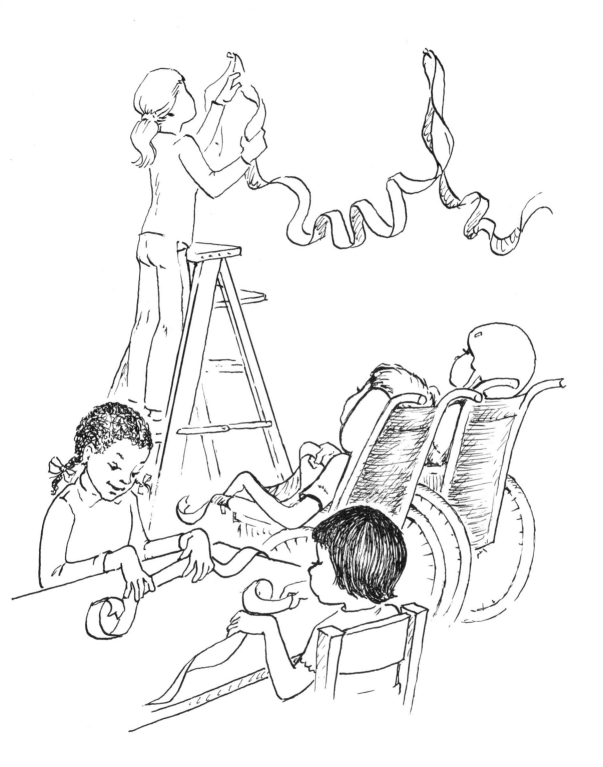

Kevin and Brian played a computer rocket game using the switch. First Don, then Jill, Mom, Dad and Grandpa tried. Kevin beat everybody but Dad.

"That's OK, Dad! I lost fair and square," Kevin said.

He raced cars in the pool with Don. His car went around the trees and under the bridge. Don's just banged the trees and turned over under the bridge.

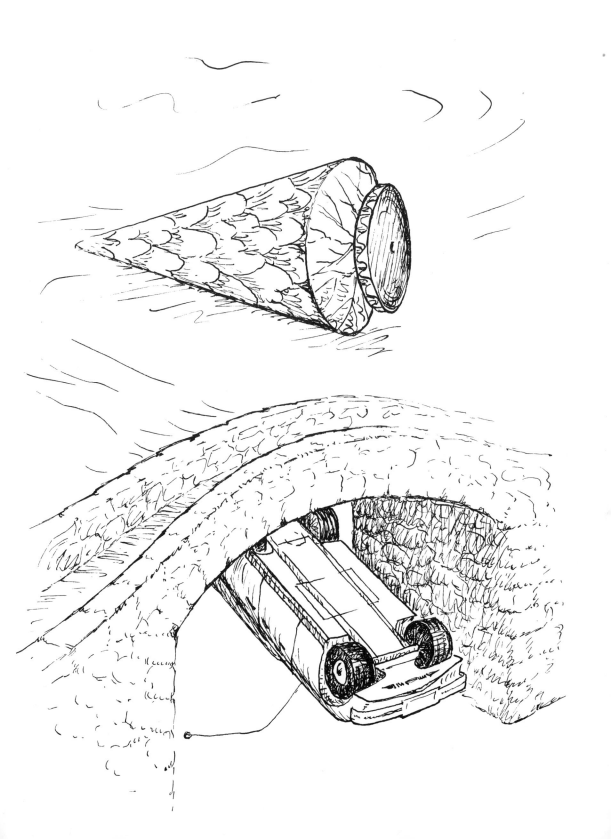

"Look everybody," Don said. "He's good. He makes that car really move!"

"You can learn to do it, too," Kevin answered. "All it takes is work!"

On the very next day Kevin felt very
happy because he knew he could win a game
— fair and square!